Solace:

Writing, Refuge, and LGBTQ Women of Color

Solace:

Writing, Refuge, and LGBTQ Women of Color

Eds. S. Andrea Allen and Lauren Cherelle

Clayton, NC

Printed in the United States of America

First Printing, 2017

Cover art and design: Lauren Curry

Paperback ISBN-13: 978-0-9972439-6-3
ePub ISBN-13: 978-0-9972439-5-6

Library of Congress Control Number: 2016913556

BLF Press
PO Box 833
Clayton, NC 27520

www.blfpress.com

For Sakia.

Table of Contents

Table of Contents

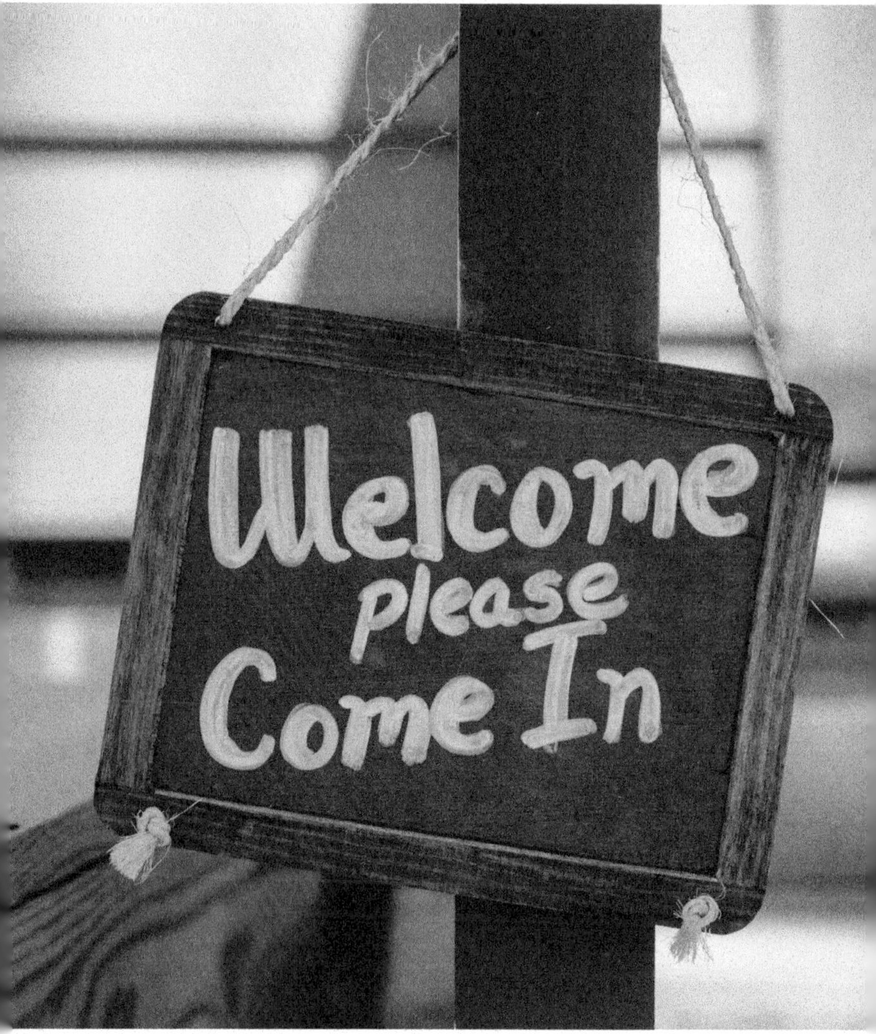
Welcome
please
Come In

Preface

When we envisioned this project last year, our hopes were high. We were forming another opportunity for Black lesbian and queer women of color to publish and press forward in their literary journeys. And this time around, we'd invite storytellers, poets, and essayists to contribute to the publication. After releasing the call for submissions, we could not have imagined the pain and loss that would encompass LGBTQ communities in 2016. Our communities gasped in collective horror at the Pulse nightclub shooting in Orlando, Florida, where 49 LGBTQ persons were murdered and dozens more injured, allegedly by someone conflicted by his own desires. We've watched state legislatures enact policies and laws designed to dehumanize us and legalize discrimination against our personhood. At this writing, 23 trans*persons have been murdered this year, an unprecedented number for this population. How is this being allowed to happen, in the land of the free and the home of the brave?

As a community, where can we find solace from the microaggression and violence enacted upon us on a daily basis? How do we amass the hope that heals our wounds as we traverse a world that seeks to destroy or repress and suppress us, simply for daring to live our truth? Who dares to shield us from the constant barrage of hatred and disdain that we face in our communities, at our places of employment, in our own families and homes?

Some of these questions are answered in this book by voices throughout North America. The poems and essays shared in this collection represent our attempts to verbalize our pain, our fear, our striving, and yes, our joy. The 13 writers and poets within these pages have laid themselves bare; reopening old wounds and reliving past heartbreaks. The result at times is a cathartic release; we are cleansed, healed, and able to start anew. We are also reminded that sometimes solace comes from within. Sometimes, solace is found in the cocoon of our relationships. Sometimes, solace only comes when we create the platforms for others to speak.

Paper Doll
Nik Nicholson

How is it
you always find me?
No matter where I am
no matter how long it's been.

You are always broken.
I am careful
not to wound you
with questions, demands
or ultimatums.

I have a gift
for handling fragile things
fragile beings.
You are a cracked jar
of grains
needing to be planted
nurtured

to grow again.
You feel safe
in my hands.
but I am just a pot
a potter
a piece of clay.
And your energy
our energy
combined
can't be contained.
Holding you
is difficult.
We're so powerful
our union
feels like a mistake.
I worry
I'll lose pieces of you.
and break
trying to sustain.

I ignore you.
turn off my phone
answer your texts
every other day

using silence as space
in an attempt to create
a foundation
to build on
a home
a barrier, a basement
of concrete and stone prayers
clarity, goals and affirmations
focus
and routine meditations.
attempting to secure
an emotional and mental state that's sacred.
Where my spirit can take refuge
from you.
A cyclone
destroying everything
in its way.

You say
you want me
I need you
to have yourself.
You always belong to someone else
you are running from.

Intuition says
you don't want me.
what do you want?
What can you give me?
With your intangible hypothetical self.
I'm tired
of being a healer
I need healing
and protection, too.
Sadly, mostly from you.
I don't want your thankless gift
of wounds
bones need skin, too.
I don't want to be another bridge
between lost, searching and found.

Still
you coax me
to look at you.
I find relativity in our wounds.
How do we bind roots
of dysfunction
when our beings
are eminent domain?

Condemned
how do we get beyond
being spiritually estranged
after we've learned
to curse ourselves
in God's name?
Forced to leave
our marrow behind
how do we reside
outside toxic ideas and behaviors
reinforced and affirmed
in our struggle to survive
clandestine depression
in desolate commuter towns?

I tell you
pain is a blessing
some cannot feel.
I tell you
there are different kinds of death
different kinds of absences
my voice echoes inside your abyss.
You are never here, to hear
walking dead
yourself.

Committed
I use my powers
imagine you whole
the way I see images
on blank canvases.
I fill you in
with all your possibilities.
I tell you
you could be an ocean landscape
with all the warm hues
of a sunset horizon
rays of light
illuminating your infinite darkness
warming the creatures
you harbor and hold at bay.

You never actually say
"save me"
but you always find me
when you're out of breath
drowning.
You have too much pride
to call me an island.

Still
you use me
to anchor yourself.
Knowing it is my nature
to pull you in
create you anew.
But I don't want my last brush stroke
to be our end.

You swear we're lovers.
I swear we are strange
strangers
most times, you're a war torn village
and I am your shaman
calling spirits
back from the dead.

This time
I don't want to Doun Doun Ba for you
my limbs and hips won't be flailing
in silence
our ancestors won't riot
on your being half

I won't go alone to ask
them for you.
This artist is tired
of kneading you, Clay.
You are too far gone to play
drums from your whole being
your percussion is hollow
your breathing is shallow
why just exist in the past or future
we're dying in this moment?
Well meaning
you sacrifice well-being
to be in the margins
of an illusion of freedom.
I don't want to stomp up earth
interceding
between all of your selves.
I don't want to conjure you back
I don't want to wait for you.
I don't want to teach you rhythms
you already know
because you're too oblivious
to maintain the flow.
You always forget

when I call
you should answer.
Last time
I gave you light
texture and depth
as your creator
I fashioned you after myself.
I gave you breath.
you as always
lacking self
awareness
and arrogant
stood erect heaving
disappearing
completely
some version of a self
you could believe in.

"Gays are going to hell:" A Lesbian Teacher Tries to Teach Compassion

Kendra N. Bryant

Tuesday, my writing students and I discussed Thomas Chatterton Williams's essay "As Black As We Wish to Be," which explores race identity and biracial people's obligation to claim their Black ethnicity. Williams' essay—excerpted from his 2011 memoir *Losing My Cool: Love, Literature, and A Black Man's Escape from the Crowd*—interrogates interracial couples and the free expression their mixed race children are afforded: "Mixed-race blacks have an ethical obligation to identify as black," says Williams, "and interracial couples share a similar moral imperative to inculcate certain ideas of black heritage and racial identity in their mixed-race children, regardless of how they look."

According to Williams, (who appears to be a White man), because Blacks have long been, and still are, oppressed and denigrated by the White American majority, "the black community can and does benefit directly from the contributions and continued allegiance of its mixed-race members, and it benefits in ways that far outweigh the private joys of freer self-expression." Williams concludes his essay by comparing his notions to those expressed in Tony Judt's 2010 autobiographical essay, "Toni." In it, Judt, a Jewish essayist, asks:

"We acknowledge readily enough our duties to our contemporaries; but what of our obligations to those who came before us?"

My writing students engaged in critical discussion regarding Williams's ideas by way of the critical thinking questions at the end of the essay. One of the questions that stumped my *Improving Writing* students was worded thusly:

> *1. Williams makes a parallel of his own pre-dicament of identification to that of Jewish self-identification. What other groups or races might have a similar predicament, and how might it differ from that of Williams?*

In an effort to assist students in both comprehending the question and reaching beyond their immediate text for answers, I asked them to consider the LGBTQ community. As a self-identified lesbian, the LGBTQ community was my first thought regarding an oppressed group of people, some of whom— like members of mixed races—can choose to live in a free expression that does not necessarily tether them to homophobic behaviors. All the students— circa 22 of them—claimed that the "LGBTQ" acronym was a foreign term. After explaining to students what "LGBTQ" stood for, I asked them whether those belonging to the LGBTQ community share a similar predicament as Williams, and if so, or not, explain.

While I anticipated light bulbs to illuminate from my Black students— most of whom come from impoverished spaces— hell broke loose instead.

"No," they emphatically said. "No, members of the LGBTQ community do not share a predicament that mirrors Williams's because in the Bible...(Fill in the blank with every verse that applies here).

With shoddily memorized Bible verses in tow, my Black sophomore, junior, and senior students— our future leaders and caretakers— exclaimed:

> Gays are going to hell!
> Gays shouldn't have children.
> Gays shouldn't be allowed to adopt children.
> Gays shouldn't be allowed to get married.
>
> I ain't with that gayness.
> Gays choose to be gay.

> "But White people dehumanized Blacks," I told them. "Slave masters kept Black men and women from marrying each other, from having and keeping their own children. And the Bible, that piece of literature written and translated and translated and translated and translated by man, was used to maintain Black subservience and to justify slavery."

> "But it's not the same," my students replied. "We were born Black, and the Bible says…"

I had never facilitated a classroom discussion that felt so grounded in hate and ignorance. While I appreciate and invite student opinion and debate, what I cannot stomach is judgment and condemnation supported by slipshod Biblical recitations. I left class feeling emotionally drained. Heavy. Sad. Uncertain. Disappointed, too.

Where was the compassion in my classroom?

Throughout the semester, we had read Martin Luther King's 1958 "An Experiment in Love," Jo Goodwin Parker's 1971 "What Is Poverty?" and Amiri Baraka's 2002 "Somebody Blew Up America." We'd listened to Nikki Giovanni lecture; we hand wrote letters to our fourth grade pen pals; and we watched Harold Cronk's 2014 *God's Not Dead* as well as King's 1963 "I Have A Dream" speech. But my consideration of LGBTQ rights transformed warm souls into cold hearts, opened minds to shut eyes, and loving language to hateful speech. My students were so grounded in their religious doctrine that they seemingly could not see the "other" as they had been seeing themselves.

Students made no considerations for other classroom students who may secretly identify as gay or lesbian. (And there were two gay students enrolled in the course—one was absent that day, and the other, wearing an ROTC uniform, remained silent.) My students clearly had not been acquainted with the Bayard Rustins, the James Baldwins, and the Alice Walkers who defended, promoted, and dedicated their life's work to civil rights—to their (my students') rights. And my gay bashing students were definitely ignorant of their professor's lesbian identity. Or maybe they did not care. Maybe they believed I should go to Hell, that I didn't have the right to marry or adopt children. Maybe they believed I *chose* to be lesbian. And so what if I did?

So today, I entered the classroom "with a charge to keep." Strapped with a 40-minute video titled "The Shadows of Hate" from *Teaching Tolerance: A Project of the Southern Poverty Law Center*, 22 handouts defining and explicating opinions, excerpted from Robert Atwan's 2013 "The Persuasive Writer: Expressing Opinions with Clarity, Confidence, and Civility," and a list of Bible verses about passing judgments and loving thy neighbor, I marched into the classroom enthusiastic about teaching tolerance and determined to teach love. I was even ready to lay myself up for an offering. However, after watching the tolerance video—whose narrator thoroughly explicated how White folks' hateful opinions of the Native American, the Chinese, Japanese, Mexican, African-American, and the Jew led to hateful speech and eventually hateful action—most of my students could not realize the condemnation and judgment expressed through their homophobia. I asked my students whether they could see their attitudes reflected in those of White people who imposed their opinions on human rights, and my students said they could not. "We don't lynch gay people," they said. "Plus, according to the Bible…"

I knew students would return to the Bible.

And so, I read about eight Biblical verses, including the often quoted Matthew 7:2–4: "For in the way you judge, you will be judged; and by your standard of measure, it will be measured to you. 'Why do you look at the speck that is in your brother's eye, but do not notice the log that is in your own eye?' Or how can you say to your brother, 'Let me take the speck out of your eye,' and behold, the log is in your own eye?" And then I asked my students how could they judge others when their God has forewarned them about hypocrisy and lawmaking? "There is only one Lawgiver and Judge, He who is able to save and to destroy," I recited from James 4:12. And I continued: "But who are you to judge your neighbor?"

"But," said one of my students, "in the Bible it says man should not lie with man," and so on. Sigh.

Reviewing the handout, and sharing my Biblical verses, the majority of my students sat there quietly, just staring at me (like the "unamused emoticon"). Most did not engage discussion, while a couple defended their positions; one student apologized for having an opinion at all. Sadly, most of my students were under the impression that I believed their *having* opinions was wrong.

I ended class feeling defeated.

I tried so hard to express my concerns with students without imposing my own political beliefs on them. But I might have failed. I'm sure I did. I mean, I want students to have their opinions, but I also want them to question EVERYTHING. I want them to identify with religion, race, class, and gender, but I want them to be loosely attached to their identifications so that their notions don't ooze into condemnation (of themselves and others). I want them to be cognizant and conscience, not ignorant and close-minded. To be compassionate and considerate, not selfish and hateful. I mean, really, how could these brazenly Christian students forget that Jesus Christ was crucified because of other folk's opinions of him?

* * *

I had every intention of coming out to my students, since they seemed to be unaware of my lesbian identity. But I didn't. I didn't fear their responses or anything like that. However, after that day's discussion—which was more like my class lecture—I felt that my fundamental lesson would be lost upon my students. I didn't want them to focus on my sexuality nor to assume my hurt feelings. And I definitely didn't want them to be sorry for having and sharing their opinions.

All I want/ed, really, was for my students to engage themselves in a contemplative inquiry that ultimately conjures their compassion for all others, human and non-human.

I don't know whether I accomplished my goal that day. However, I'm going to rest in the notion that people will come to understanding when it is time for them to understand. I believe Christians call that, amazing grace. And so, it is.

"...what I cannot stomach is judgment
        and condemnation supported by
                slipshod Biblical recitations."

Queer Brown Girl
Eunice Sierra-Gonzalez

I like your hands
the way they
grasp your dreams
firmly.

The way they hold my heart
gently
the way they write
poetry through your
ambition.

I like your hands
the way they illustrate a love
for yourself
the way they fiddle
when you're nervous
when I
make you nervous

because I do,
I see you,
queer brown girl.

I see your closet, too.
how it coddles you,
how you're afraid to let it go,
how you're afraid to come out of it
because rejection hurts more
than loneliness.

I see your closet,
the way it keeps you warm,
the way it protects you
from the pain of
losing all you've ever known,
all you've ever loved.

I see the way you want to love,
same gender love,
passionately
and
honestly,
and finally, raw.

I see you, queer brown girl.
grasping yourself,
trying to fight the urge to
be queer,
be brown,
and be you.

I've been there.
But I'm here, now.
here for you.
the door is open for whenever
you want to come out
and into
me.

born provocative: *a collage*
librecht baker

i.
born provocative with buried rituals
an heiress to an unknown culture colored
my conglomerate, a civilization drawing water
from river with abundance bundled in head
while dilating birthrights' passage
and humming spirituals bursting from sutures
    old patterns aren't meant to be new skin
i remember to remember
i remember to remember
i remember to remember
    with this knowing, i call my name
slick with parting lips' spit of herstories
    with this knowing, i have a name
coagulated monthly moon blood
    with this knowing, i drip my names
from shadows borderland parables

so others of us can midwife
the others of us whose wombs portal
the others of us into the hands of
others of us catching
the others of us as we birth
the others of us

ii.

as we birth the others of us
our memories reach back
summoning old speak so we spit new tongue
    a dialogue of mud & white magnolia flowers
learning to water ourselves from earth's
    roots upward
we've become a diaspora salvaging paradise
    inside cement cities
speaking feral beliefs through our inner chambers
of solar symphonies
we festivals their premeditated funerals for us
    our collective visibility triumphs
when we summon
the spirit of undoing past patterns
we stage refusals
against myths attempting to statistic us chaotic

they can't stuff us inside chaos that only exists
because chaos can't contain us
our breath becomes unbound pamphlets
fluttering in zephyr winds
ensuring our dreams find our seeking
as we seek dreams spun within us

iii.
born provocative with buried rituals
an heiress to an unknown culture colored
my conglomerate, a civilization drawing water
from river with abundance bundled in head
    rising from bone black bones
    from fire's ash
we are no burning phoenix rising
    our energy is etheric – ripples of healing
    dilate and negotiate language's space
with these bodies spilling across identities
us kind
forage a vision with our bodies' waters
    what have we done with these bodies
breathe within our primordial waters
    what are we doing with these bodies
coloring in legacies' lacy accents

what have we done to deserve these bodies
transmit the medicine of our nations
as we chant ascension from false decay
of these bodies
our bodies
the others of us inside
these bodies

iv.
the others of us mining
the gaps in invisible and gentrified spaces
awakening these bodies
making passage with precedent
locating our presence within the present
carving theories with restless urges
drafting resistance to oppression
building epistemologies
with western, northern, eastern and southern
african aboriginal rhythms
we center our darken, light bodies
black matter of worlds
coming out of worlds
coming out of worlds
where the sun comes

into our lap
as moonlight drips
    patter
    patter
drips from pussies
speaking home
to the legacies
of precolonial africa
colored/ negro
black/ african-american
black-american/ black
womanist/ feminist
duality of multiple identities
shifting, queering
american ramblings
as we pray with internalized silence
to which we were born to
bury and séance
elevating crones
who birth maidens
who birth mothers
holding ceremony
so the others of us remember
to make offerings

to those of us who forgot
to offer ourselves
to ourselves and shift
the legacies undulating within
    and so it is
àse

"I don't want to be invisible."

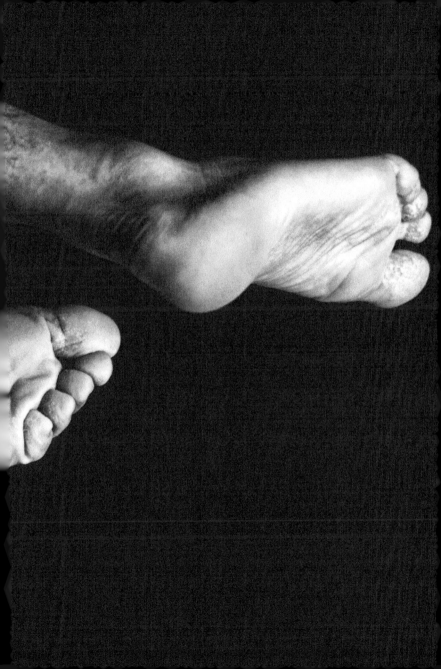

Push Back and Breathe
M. Shelly Conner

Last year when I proposed to my girlfriend, she broke up with me. The proposal itself felt like quite the accomplishment. As a black, queer woman, it can be a feat to achieve even the most basic of liberties. Proposing to my girlfriend felt like I had finally made it to the mountaintop, only to then tumble backwards, free falling into the unknown. To be fair, and also quote an uncle's response when I asked whether he'd fallen off the wagon of sobriety, I was pushed.

Not so much by the woman who no longer wanted to be with me—although that is not irrelevant to the point. In fact, I think I wanted to marry a woman for the same reason that I strove to get a PhD and seek publication for my novel. These are great accomplishments for anyone, but very difficult with the added marginalization of race, gender, and sexuality.

Thirteen days after my break up, I was watching a TED Talk. The presenter, a middle-aged white woman, was recounting having to overcome her stutter and other insecurities in order to open herself up to opportunities. Apparently, there are a wealth of opportunities waiting for folks if they just believe in themselves and are willing to come out of their shells for a bit. Then I re-read Kiese Laymon's brilliant excerpt from "How to Slowly Kill Yourself and Others in America" and I was quickly returned to reality. For those of us who are multiply marginalized, opening ourselves up often runs the risk of social ostracization, political persecution, and police brutality. The TED Talk lady's advice, although theoretically sound (what I like to call privileged advice like "leaning in"), is about as useful to me as the YouTube lady who demonstrates the proper method for folding fitted bed sheets while stating, "One of the biggest challenges you will face *in your life* is how to fold a fitted sheet" (emphasis mine). Must be nice, lady.

Laymon writes about wanting to push back against that impenetrable force that corrals black folk into our proper places—docile, non-threatening, unaccomplished. This push back reminds me of when Toni Morrison boldly proclaimed that she writes for black folk; Janelle Monáe tweeted that her body is not for male consumption; and my teachings to a predominately white class of university freshman about how African American texts "talk back" to mainstream works while pushing their own aesthetic. I also think of the peaceful protests as well as the rioting associated with the Black Lives Matter movement. Black rage is the antithesis of white privilege; and as long as the latter exists, so shall the former. I wonder what the TED Talk lady would say about overcoming the insecurities around the constant awareness and reminders that my life as a black woman in 2017 is worth less than it would have been in 1817.

I carry this burden when I enter mainstream queer communities that fight for marriage equality yet ignore that many queer people of color are struggling, as I am, with the load of racial and economic inequality. And yes, I clearly want to marry—although my obstacles are more personal than legal; but it seems considerably irrelevant by comparison to those who are struggling for basic human rights, like the right to life. I do not understand any LGBTQ movement for equality that does not address in its agenda the violence enacted upon queer people of color; the rate of homelessness, incarceration, and detention among queer youth of color; and racism within the LGBTQ community.

My marriage proposal was in part a push back. I was in love and I made a very public showing of it. Friends and family always advise against being too public on social media. They label it attention-seeking. I guess it's a simple and easy assessment. Truthfully, I publicized key highlights of my relationship for the same reason Toni Morrison wrote *The Bluest Eye*—because there weren't (many) examples of such a thing. For me, I just wanted to demonstrate affirming, black queer love for those seeking it; those who've never seen it; and for straight family and friends who couldn't conceive of it.

Social media timelines and feeds bleed daily examples of misogynoir from Black men (as in the beating death of Joyce Quaweay by her boyfriend and his friend for "not submitting"). We see it in the Texas police officer that slammed a black, bikini-clad teenager to the ground at a McKinney pool party. It looks like Daniel Holtzclaw, the Oklahoma City police officer who raped black women while on duty. But it's not just present in the most overt acts of violence. Black women are harassed from street corners, cars, and social venues by men who feel entitled to their smiles, conversation, body, and time. Zora Neale Hurston wrote that black women are the mules of the world, and truer words have not been spoken.

In this climate, black women loving each other—openly and honestly—is one of the most radical acts that can be done. I don't subscribe to the notion of not declaring things out of fear of losing or jinxing them. If my lost love had anything to do with my public and private celebrations of it, then it was not right for me– one who has learned to celebrate all aspects of life. I do this as much for myself as I do it for the slain soldiers of the movement who've been robbed of their opportunities.

Same sex marriage is a personal exercise of freedom; yet to love as a black queer woman is what Audre Lorde accurately described in stating,

"Caring for myself is not self-indulgent, it is self-preservation, and that is an act of political warfare." I struggle with the notion of how much to display and share with my community. It is largely informed by how lost I felt when I first searched for black queer sisterhood—sometimes invisible (quite possibly by design) to those outside of it.

I don't want to be invisible. I don't always want to be an example, but don't always have a choice. I am still in awe to see black women together and in love. I wanted to join the ranks, much in the way I hope to see my novel alongside the works of Morrison, Walker, and Lorde. Not only is it my personal life's work, it is my contribution to the social justice movement. As much as my writing may speak to colleagues and peers, my hope is that it finds some skinny, black queer girl in a classroom and whispers love to her while instructing how to fashion a pen into a sword.

People who advocate keeping to yourself, head down and in private don't realize that this is how we teach black folk to survive. Don't bring too much attention to yourself and what you have. This is how we have come to self-restrict. We now participate in our own confinement—Laymon's slow killing of others and ourselves.

Not only should I be able to fall in love, but I should also be able to shout it from tops of Mt. Facebook. And not just for those who have thanked me for sharing positive images of black queer life and love, for which we are clearly aching (as evidenced by our support of everything black and queer from Viola Davis' same sex love in *How to Get Away with Murder* to the Prancing Elite dance team). I may have posted pics of our two faces happy to be smiling in front of each other as a public placeholder for the non-existence of a black Modern Family or Will and Grace; but I also did this for myself, as my right.

I wonder what it would be like to go through the experience of romantic heartbreak without the added anxiety of racial oppression, gender inequality, and homophobia. I think of mainstream books like *Eat, Pray, Love* with protagonists who can dash off to other countries to heal their wounds. Still, I have to admire my tenacity and resilience, else I see it as naïveté and foolishness. That beneath the rhetoric of inequality, beneath even the harsh experiences of inequality, beneath the personal heartache—I do live my life like the TED Talk lady suggests: unabashedly opening myself to opportunities.

Yet in the same vein, being open to the knocks and bruises of being black and queer and female. Living my life and striving for my dreams is my push back. I don't know whether it makes me more free or alive. It certainly hurt like hell during my breakup. Sometimes my breath catches in my chest and I don't know whether it will release itself. Then I think about Natasha McKenna struggling for her last breath and her final words to the police as she was repeatedly tasered while in restraints: *You said you wouldn't kill me.* And I realize that not only can I breathe, but I must breathe.

Hymn
Sheila Tartaglia

My heart—that wild bird—beats
her plumes against a cage of bone.

Of late, the nearness of spring
reminds her of how the wind tastes
as it carries her aloft.

Is it late? Is it late? Is it late?
Her wings beat in a syncopated rhythm
as she mimics flight, asleep.

It is not late, spring whispers back
bending the naked branches of March,
buds rising like goose bumps.

My heart—that wild bird—beats
her plumes against the night sky—
the cage of bone was only a dream.
Spring is filling her cup.

A blazing harvest moon
lowers, and fills, and swings nightly,
like a pendulum, keeping her up.

Finding Refuge, Finding Home
Eunice Gonzalez-Sierra

When Ma found out about Lucia and what she had done to me, she swore there'd be a man out there that could love me the way I deserved, the way any woman deserved. I didn't tell Ma much about the way Lucia made me feel—about the way she made me love again and how truly wonderful it was to finally feel like myself, a queer woman of color that had the capacity to love and be loved by another woman. Ma grew up in a small *pueblito* in Oaxaca, Mexico. Where women were taught that love was having dinner ready for your husband, that love was bearing children and never once complaining about how hard it was to be both a woman and brown. I learned early in life that my mother deserved more, that my mother, like most women of color, was getting ripped off on the politics of love. Cupid was cheating them, he was cheating us—like most men in our family did. I learned early on that my life wouldn't revolve around a man. I learned there was a cycle that had to be broken because it was not made with us in mind.

I come from a woman who grows strawberries for a living, who gets paid (very minimally) to make this world a sweeter place. And she has. She's made me sweet despite how bitter I've wanted to become. Despite how hidden I've kept this part of myself—the part who wanted to love and be loved authentically. My mother has always been the woman of my dreams, which is why I refuse to settle for a man who will never love the way my mother has. Which is why I am nearly certain my place is with a woman.

Lucia was magical. In retrospect, I gave her too much credit. But I want to talk about her the way I remembered her— kindly. Her skin was sweet as *pan dulce*, the white kind, not the brown kind, but still sweet nonetheless. She had a way of thinking that made my head spin. Lucia taught me things I never knew. She taught me about the bond between two women that wanted to love one another (or rather wanted to be loved by one another, I eventually learned this). My heart (my injured, resilient, little heart) knows that Lucia and I could've made it far. If she was just a little stronger, if she cared a little more—but she didn't. I do have to say, her skin was our kryptonite, our downfall. It's hard to love a brown body when hers is white. It's hard to love a big body when hers is small. Lucia decided it was hard to love me. But not because I was hard to love, but because life was made easy for her. It's made easy for most who possess some sort of whiteness, who wear it on their skin...proudly. I don't blame Lucia for not loving me. If anything, I thank her. I learned to love myself because she couldn't. And now, my queer brown body loves no one more than itself. Loves no one more than the brown body that keeps it warm.

Ma told me Lucia didn't deserve me anyway. She said I'd find a man to love me the way I deserved, and I wondered, *the way Pa loved you?* The way he loved the other women he saw in times of insecurity and resentment? Pa wasn't a bad man, or maybe patriarchy is making me believe this even when I know deeply he was empty. Patriarchy has a way of making women believe that men deserve forgiveness; that they deserve consideration; that they deserve all that we seldom receive from them.

Despite my feminism now, I truly feel bad for the way *machismo* has ruined my father, the way it has made him empty and sad. I know there's a heart in there, hollow, but beating. I know he's sorry and I know he's sad. I will love him, but I don't know whether committing to another man in my life is within my capacity. I deserve more, and after all, Ma always deserved more.

Pa grew up thinking that alcohol was the magical cure to all his problems. My mother and him argued—he drank. He became nostalgic—he drank. He was stressed or tired or lonely—he drank. He sought refuge in a bottle of *Patron*; a bottle that would abandon him once dawn came creeping. I've told my father about Lucia, and how she hurt me. He said, "basta con tantas pendejadas;" stop with all the bullshit. My father refuses to believe that I have the capacity to love a woman. I saw it in his eyes when I revealed the news that love came in the form of a lean, tall, mixed woman. Mixed like the swirls of *pan dulce*, white and brown and somehow so very sweet—despite it all. But this isn't about Lucia, or the way she loved and left me. This is about the way my brown body has chosen to love, unapologetically, honestly and sometimes passionately. And even though this type of love may sometimes be questioned (often times, actually), it exists, and it is valid and it is real. A love between women is valid; a love between women of color is revolution. I've chosen to live by Gloria Anzaldúa's words when truly trying to understand my connection to other women. *"As a mestiza, I have no homeland, my country cast me out; yet all countries are mine because I am every woman's sister or potential lover."* Beautifully crafted to describe how wonderful it is to be a queer woman of color. To know that we're all bound to have a connection with other women, to know that we belong everywhere we go because there is a need for women's solidarity all over the world—and in all over ourselves and within each other.

Now, I love another woman, much more than the first. A brown woman, with the blood of Oaxaca, Mexico flowing through her veins, curves so dangerous you have to hit the breaks a little just to be safe, long brown hair and red lipstick to show the boys she's not to be messed with. She's a woman that taught herself how to love through finding her mother, through finding her mother's strength. This woman lives inside me. This woman finally learned how to love herself before the curse of patriarchy and self-sabotage. (Why do we do that to ourselves?) And how often have women learned to do just this? To find refuge in oneself? To find solace within oneself? I have. It took a while, but I finally have. I'm finally home. It feels nice to be loved, raw.

"A love between women is valid; a love between women of color is revolution."

Pummel
Hala Aurangzeb

So you hit her,
and the world becomes a little better,
fairer,
now you have a power
over
someone.

But did it bring
back the string
of jobs; the ring
of friends, roaring,
in laughter, again?
Did it bring
the offer
of dignity, here;
the stirrings
of passion, here;

the promise of
good times to come, here?
Here, in the belly of the
White Man.

She used to
take the blue
off you—
help you
shrug it off,
slide it down,
and she'd hang it
careful
on the coat rack.
For tomorrow.
Now who
will slew
in the dirt
with you?
Now who
will coo,
in your pain,
with you?
Now who will still

the world
and fill
the silence
until
spring breathes again?
Now she
cringes in the corner
as you enter
the door.

It is too dark to scream now?
Do you hear it better when she does
it for you?

An Awakening as a Spiritual Activist

Eliana Buenrostro

"When stress is overwhelming, you shut down
   your feelings, plummet into depression
   and unremitting sorrow."

~ Gloria Anzaldúa

The Coatlicue State

I underwent my first coatlicue state during my
second year at UCLA. I was 21, kind of a reckless—
definitely unorganized—organizer and I was drow-
ning in my convictions, study habits that never
developed and a then undiagnosed mental illness.
I got sick over and over and I had to keep leaving
school for weeks and quarters. At the time, I was

taking a class entitled "Border Consciousness" and all I could keep thinking about was how I couldn't even do all the work required for a class that incorporated heavy use of Anzaldúa concepts. Anzaldúa, who was ultimately failed by academia and died from cancer when she was a teaching assistant at a UC. I literally lit candles to her spirit as I struggled to finish the quarter.

An abusive relationship was the thing that sent me over the edge. I had never in my life experienced a depressive episode that bad. I want to pretend like I don't have the mental space for it, but I still have triggers and I still have nightmares. I've never been forced to analyze myself so closely before and all the truths I unknowingly held dear. Student organizing spaces can be some of the most toxic and chaotic institutions on college campuses. I remember giving a presentation on patriarchy in the Latinx community during an organization meeting while I was in an abusive relationship. I thought the feeling of shame would never leave.

Letting Go

All I remember of my last quarter at UCLA was how badly I wanted to drop out and how much I wanted to be rescued from my despair. Unsurprisingly, that rescue never came and I packed my bags for a semester abroad in México. I remember I was terrified and there were so many times when I thought I would withdraw from the program. My fatigue was taking its toll on my spirit. Before departing South, I went to the doctor so many times in the hopes of finding a cure, an explanation, anything (actually, I still haven't found it). I remember my overwhelming sense of grief. It was like I never knew anything but grief. I couldn't remember myself before my trauma. I was a completely different and my inner light had just gone out. I started taking antidepressants and I moved in cautious small steps. I fell over and over and over. Fear paralyzed me from time to time. That was not a new revelation. I found it hard to enjoy my family's company in my state.

Now let us shift..."the path of conocimiento... inner work, public acts"

I have meditated a lot on the subject of healing. Wondering where it would take me. It has taken many different forms over time. Most recently, I have redirected that energy inward. Letting it quell the flames that had taken over my brain for the past two years of my life. Reading Gloria Anzaldúa's conception of a spiritual activist was what finally manifested the bridge between healing and academia for me. Thinking of myself as a healer started to click. I knew academia was never going to save me, so I started meticulously crafting that space that would. I began to feel very detached from organizing since its toxicity had made sick and scared in the first place. After leaving a triggering space, I was able to take an active role in healing myself from my trauma. I still don't think I want to go back to organizing. It could happen someday, but I'm not holding my breath. Instead, I have learned to be a spiritual activist and to channel energy into the spaces that can be more accepting of me as a fluid and mentally ill Chicana.

I spoke to women everyday that had been through hell and back. They were on a journey to heal just like me. Every single day my fatigue and anxiety threatened to overwhelm me, but I fought back. I learned to work through my demons and in the process I helped others with theirs. I had no idea that my own trauma would be the catalyst to transform my soul and my path. I studied and I lived healing and I was finally able to pass on that knowledge to someone else. Every week I communed with *mujeres chiapanecas. Mujeres indígenas y mestizas.* We cried, grieved, and shared together. I was lifted.

When I returned from Chiapas, one of my professors told me I looked radiant. I think that has been the most full I've ever felt in my life. I felt some of sort of makeshift peace, my skin full of stress breakouts, but glowing nonetheless. The glow from presenting my traumas to a room of my peers and the glow from a *limpia* to celebrate the end of my academic career. I told a room of my peers what I had been through.

Healing became the mantra that I injected into every aspect of my life and especially into my research project and the workshops I facilitated. I read in *This Bridge Called My Back* Gloria Anzaldúa's interview with Luisah Teish and her earth charm to match her growth with a plant's. I tracked my progress through the growth of a plant I bought from a vendor in the streets of San Cristóbal de las Casas. I diligently worked on my writing, setting out to heal something in me, anything. The plant grew and, eventually, it outgrew its pot. Even when I moved it to a bigger container, I observed it from the bottom and all the roots looked so constrained. They needed room to spread. Before leaving Chiapas, I left it in the care of a good friend who works at the women's center where I volunteered.

My time away has given me so much life. It doesn't feel right to say that I have gotten my life back because I haven't. I'm not sure that the person I was is even me anymore. Trauma is scary in that it transforms every ounce of your being. I am revitalized, and despite still needing to make choices based on past hurts, I am still here and I am still fighting.

"Academia was never going to save me."

Going Back Home
Sheila Tartaglia

Here, bricks undulate
with green ivy leaves
large as hands.
I grew up here
a generation ago
when the urban garden
my parents sowed
fed us all season. Up, up
I climb the creaking stairs,
holding swollen wood banisters
worn smooth as tusk.
Our tin-tiled, turn of the century
hall winds along floors,
past numbered doors,
up, up, to the top floor,
with a pyramid skylight

diffused in celestial blue.
Home—father and mother
welcome me as it was in the beginning,
world without end. We sup
at the simple table,
we three now healed
in the kitchen of years.
All my days
I will recall them clearest:
Father, Atlas,
shouldering our world,
Mother, Madonna,
her burning heart revealed.

"Where do words come from?
The gods of solace, child.
The gods of solace."

Remedios
Almah LaVon Rice

I lie beside my lover after love. Tongues have just threaded us, thrummed us to one high note. And yet…the skin is sealed. The scent of abrasions is in the air. Nothing really gave way—just the slippage of orgasm, the mudslide to mute. I put my ear between her breasts and I can hear what sustains her, far and faint. Inscrutable heart. There are ways to outwit the body's self-possession: mouth, ear, anus. Or through poetry. To sing the body open. That illegible body.

* * *

"Language is the only homeland."
– Czesław Miłosz

* * *

More than a lover's body, more than my mother's body, I have been most relentlessly bonded to and bound by books. The arbor of words. When my mother would send me out to play with neighborhood kids, I would slip a book in the waistband of my shorts and find a place out of maternal eyeshot to read in secret. So I strapped a book's spine to my own and grew taller, stronger. Yes, words held me up and still do. Or, I can re-myth the scoliosis I was diagnosed with as a child as an attempt to curve around words, language my trellis. Curve, twine, tangle: people are too cruel, too remote, too inconsistent, but within the pages of a book I can finally taste the constancy and intimacy I crave.

* * *

In the war zone of my childhood, a book was as good as a pup tent. One of my favorite writers, Carole Maso, calls it "the shelter of the alphabet." Yes.

* * *

What are my strategies for survival?

Who says I survived? Part of me died back there in the war. But some of me persisted: those remnants I dried and pressed between the pages of a book. Words preserve me.

* * *

Zami: A New Spelling of My Name was the first book to suggest what life could be like for me, a young black woman attempting to account for her desires for other women. I identified with Lorde's fat black girl exiles and her queer longing for her stony mother's embrace. I remain tattooed by the passage in which Lorde finds home in another little girl for only one heartbreaking instant–infinity— prefiguring her endless quests as an adult to find haven in the arms of women. This is a *saudade* I recognize.

Zami was also billed as a "biomythography"— a concept that, in its undistillable mystery, keeps me intrigued as a writer of creative nonfiction. Lit by Lorde's example, I have written some biomythographies of my own. Lorde urges me to keep spelling my name in a world where my personhood often seems written in invisible ink.

* * *

When I discovered the magical realism of Latin American writers as a teenager, I was swept off my feet. Up, up, up! I took to hovering near the ceiling, just like the gardenia-eating, moon-addled characters. I fell upwards in love with this literature and saw no need to come back down to the quotidian. However, for years I delayed reading arguably the most seminal text of magical realism, Gabriel García Márquez's *One Hundred Years of Solitude.* Why? Because I couldn't find an edition with the "right" typeface. Call me a font fetishist, but the shapes of letters seriously optimizes the reading experience for me. The objects of my queer desire are not limited to human or even the sentient—so I am coming out now, for the first time in print (and somewhat cheekily), as a typosexual.

* * *

Garamond is the god in my cosmology. That's not interstellar debris, but letters. Their names are Arial, look up. They fall down and are caught in the netting of woods, the ancestors of paper. Where do words come from? The gods of solace, child. The gods of solace.

* * *

There are black women writers whose holy texts solace me. Gayl Jones, from Kentucky as I am, penned "Legend," a cautionary fable of haunts and haints. Oh, the music of June Jordan's essay, "The Difficult Miracle of Black Poetry in America," flinting bright with its insights on race, voice, violence, and permission. I loved reading about orphans as a book-mad baby queer, and when I read Toni Morrison's *Beloved*, I orphaned myself just so that bloody, love-thickened Sethe would claim me as her own. Zora Neale Hurston's *Their Eyes Are Watching God* was so achingly beautiful that halfway through, I stopped and re-started the novel from the beginning because I needed to loiter and linger as long(ingly) as I could between its covers. I did the same thing with Octavia Butler's *Wild Seed* because I was blown away by a black woman who refused to be anyone's hope mammy—her gaze was as shadowed and pitiless as my own, and I found comfort, perversely, because she offered none. And if books can have daughters, A.J. Verdelle's *The Good Negress* is definitely *Their Eyes Are Watching God*'s—how I related to the central character, a black girl whose every step toward erudition and English class patson-the-head seemed to lead further away from home and family. And speaking of daughters, Carolivia Herron's *Thereafter Johnnie*: the trauma of incest tunes its lyre. In Thylias Moss' *Slave Moth*, I found an ancestor in the protagonist Varl, an enslaved girl who stitches life-saving verse to wear under her clothes.

* * *

Remedios the Beauty was a character that enthralled me in *One Hundred Years of Solitude.* What would it be like to be that guilelessly, mythically beautiful? To be so beautiful that gravity is too ensorcelled to hold onto you, so that earth loses its purchase? I have always felt decidedly earthy, inescapably corporeal, as ugly and as mundane as mud. What remedies are there for an unsightly, terminally grounded girl bookworm who isn't necessarily precious in the sight of family, neighborhood, community, and the larger black world? (Being legible to whiteness is so out of the question.) I don't really know. But I do identify as a fairy monster these days, bending myth to my purposes—and toward remedy and reparation. Lorde and Márquez gave me that.

* * *

I actually read some of *One Hundred Years of Solitude* in my brother's closet. My mother, father, and I were visiting my brother for Thanksgiving. The blaring TV and press of four people in a not-huge one-bedroom apartment sent me to retreat and read in the walk-in closet in my brother's bedroom. He eventually opened the closet door, found me there, and noted that the title of the novel was quite apt. I had to admit that it was and we shared a chuckle. It was less a laughing matter when some years later, my brother walked into my bedroom before I had a chance to spirit away the *Curve Magazine* lying on my bed. Awkward. After ages of hiding books like Paul Monette's *Becoming A Man* and Deborah Abbott's *From Wedded Wife to Lesbian Life*, my "sin" was revealed. My years of black queer girl solitude were cracked. So I learned (again) that while my cloister of stories provided comfort, it couldn't promise protection.

* * *

Despite all of the ducking and dodging as a black queerlet to avoid playing with other kids. Despite closet(ed) reading. Despite the fact a real live human has to be extraordinarily compelling to compete with the humans telling me tales between book covers. Despite all of this, I read to close the gap between lovers, planets, strands of DNA. I read for remedies.

* * *

William Nicholson: "We read to know that we are not alone."

* * *

I read to induct other landscapes, other realities, into my bloodstream. I read for intimacy, as impossible and fraught as that project tends to be. I read because I can't get close enough. I read to stay, in spite of it all. May this consolation never leave me.

*"I have been most relentlessly
    bonded to and bound by books."*

Confluence
Sheila Tartaglia

Tributaries flow into greater rivers, are forever

caught in this rush. Such sweet confluence

makes its own music, mellifluous, fluid,

a delicate melding of piano and cello

rising, cascading to a crescendo

you could feel in your toes

if you stood on the bank

where this occurs,

and heard what

a mermaid

or poet

feels.

An American Boulevard
Mica Standing Soldier

Walking my German dog down an
American road
with my Jewish fears and my Native hair.
With a crown of ice on top my burning head,
I kept a cold and quiet stare.
My purebred demanded space and I held him
with a custom collar
because my family could afford it.
We could afford vacations, cars, and therapy.

And still to the four teenagers
in a bulging jeep chanting "white power"
as if their
pink lungs were ivory,
still, to the kids
in the black jeep with the same honor roll
bumper sticker as my own,

still, I was poor and I was powerless
And I needed to know my place.
Their sharp Hitler salutes cut through my
ice crown
while my European dog warned them to stay away

At home, my Jewish mother and my Native father
forgave my brown tears because
we all remembered how it was to be weak.
And I cursed my sweatpants and baggy shirt
because too native meant too dirty meant too
much danger to walk down an American road with
my German dog.

I Been Prepared
Dr. Nubian Sun

Got bachelor's degree in Social Work
and switched myself over to get master's
degree in Social Work

So I can help folk

Learned theories, the ways to do things
and say things, techniques, mines and
your history
Learned about my oppressed self
Black
Femme
Queer
Young
Southern
Low income
Memphis-ish
Mississippi-ish
Survivor
Queen

Got a Master's degree and started seeing clients and getting them signed up for food stamps—*after I left the food stamp office from getting mines.*

Started encouraging clients to see visit their loved ones in prison—*after I left from visiting mines.*

Took clients to get food baskets from churches and get "saved" in the process—*after I got saved and got mines.*

Met with one client—a teenage girl— while she spoke to me about confronting family members who sexually abused her—*after I confronted mines.*

Took client to get abortion care in the middle of the night—*after I took a friend to get hers.*

Pawnshops and Payday Advance places used to know my name. They even called me when I got my money right to see when I was coming back.

Did intake with homeless client—*after I woke up from sleeping in my car.*

Picked up donated food for an after school program for at-risk youth—*after I drank cups of water to hush my three-day hunger pangs.*

Safety planned over the phone with a client who was hiding in the closet from her partner—*after I left the court filing a restraining order. I had an ex-girlfriend turned stalker. She threatened my life daily and vandalized my car three times.*

Switched myself over to get a doctorate degree in Social Work and started teaching folk who wanna help folk
Volunteering in the community
Writing thangs scholarly and unscholarly
Stepping into classes of myself.

Helping students to live their best selves now
See a new path in life
Stand in their truth
Not to be ashamed of their past
Let no credential or dollar amount be a wedge between you and your folks
Everyone is/has been somebody's client
No social status is ever safe from need

And they been prepared from the jump.

About Loving the Tides
Eunice Sierra-Gonzalez

When you left, heartache came knocking
at my doorstep.
I didn't open the door this time.
Then came the headache,
Turns out, I had the ocean inside me…
I needed to cry.

I was afraid that if I let the ocean out,
It'd consume me for competing with its depth.
It's a war we both would have inevitably lost.

I, for being too stubborn to learn how to swim,
and it, for consuming you in my mind, too.

I blame you for disappointing her,
for igniting the tsunami that would have
no choice,

but to swallow me whole
simply because you can't take a heart out of
a human
without it dying.

When you left,
my heart didn't break
it drowned.
Your absence
suffocating my ability to breathe
again.

There's something about the tide
that reminds me of you,
perhaps it's the way she always comes back
even when she knows her home is not with me.

There's something about the tide
that reminds me of you,
perhaps, it's the fact that she's shallow.

There's something about the tide
that reminds me of you,
out of all the parts of the ocean,
she was the only part I touched,
she was the only part I loved,
and just like you,
she always left me.

Shaped Absence

Imani Sims

She will say it
is broken stone heart:
severed granite counter tops
and skeleton in closet,

Far too many secrets
to bury me with.
The obituary will read;
Here lies medusa– sorcery–

A heart too snake
Head solstice summer to
Forget. Too black girl
Memory in Indian sea.

Confessions

Kendra N. Bryant

*(Because she said to me, "There is a door
that has been opened for someone
like you.")*

I am 36.

I've had 22 lovers.
I took my first at 17-years-old.
Or maybe she—
at 43—
took me.

I've had seven one-night/one-weekend
stands—
two of whom were men I practiced with
just to be sure I wanted women
& wasn't reacting to being molested.
I was eight, or maybe ten,
& it hurt just as much as my monthly period—

which still comes,
tho I can't have babies.

Still, two dogs are mine
& so are two nieces,
& I kiss them four on a regular basis.

I prefer pants over skirts.
I don't wear blouses,
I wear shirts.
Some claim I'm way too curt.
Others hate it when I flirt.
But I hate when folks call me a stud
or an oxymoron
or accidentally, a sir

& tho my masculine energy
feels stronger than the woman in me
I promise, I don't like fist bumps

I like whole hugs
like I like whole foods.
I want plump breasts pressed 'gainst mine

Sweet like
chocolate covered peanut M&Ms
mixed in Indiana's Kettle Corn
& washed w/ Manischewitz red wine.

&
Long like
Celie's contemplative nature
nurtured thru daily letters to Nettie & God
& consecrated w/ Shug Avery's shimmies

But sometimes I'm a pescetarian
on a 1,000 calorie diet
hoping that fish & bread are enuf.

I am afraid of being too fat
afraid to die
afraid to lose
afraid to take real chances.

I am afraid
more often than I am not.

I tattoo my body in lieu of cutting my thighs,
& I pierce my skin to feel alive.
I laugh a lot when I need to cry,
& I masturbate w/ hopes to arrive
at a door that's been opened for me.

"...since we must commune in alphabets,
let us intend to libate ourselves in reverie"

Solace in Words
Claudia Moss

Words are my panacea for most of the ills I've encountered on my life's journey. At times of sorrow and distress, I have sought solace in the written word. When my soul yearned for expression, words marshaled about me, my choice of sentry. They are my pinot grigio and my saving grace.

For as far back as I can remember, my love affair with words has thrived.

As a prepubescent girl, when playing with my siblings in our Waterbury, Connecticut backyard was no longer appealing, I discovered solace in the books I brought home by the bagful from the local library, one of my favorite places then and now. The books hummed with stories that seemed infinitely more intriguing than games of hide and seek. When I read, the sanctity of Sunday School enveloped me. Their smell, the front and back covers, the dust jacket, the blurbs, the way the pages rifled, their length, their language, whether they came with pictorials in the middle—books inspired me. Reading inserted me into another place and time, and likely, well before the final page, I'd read slower, prolonging an inevitable ending.

My mother taught me to seek solace in words.

Soft-spoken, educated, and beautiful, Mama was a reader. One who corralled my sisters, twin brother, and me around the kitchen table after dinner and bid us listen to her read stories in this magnificent voice that swept me into adventures, embroiled me in conflict, directed me to magic doors and allowed me to be my own heroine. Unbeknownst to me then, my mother's affinity for reading paved the road to my world of words today.

Sickness came to call when I was in the tenth grade at Kennedy High School. Mama had recently birthed our baby sister, so perhaps her weakness meant her body's slow rejuvenation. Not to be. My family relocated to Tuskegee, AL, where Mama took her last breath on a cot in my paternal grandparents' front room. This time sorrow called at the door of my soul. Mama, the center of all that I knew, was gone. I plunged into a vacuum of silence, burying myself in books to ease the pain, the void of her absence in my life excruciating.

Adolescent protagonists blazing trails and solving mysteries saved me. My love of words grew as I moved through adolescence, high on stories.

A man who ruled my childhood with an iron arm, my father believed in corporal discipline and the tenet that children should be seen and unheard. To meet his eyes while he was chastising was a show of disrespect and merited swift punishment, a whipping with the thick, leather belt supporting his pants. Him unbuckling it was the bane of my childhood. Daddy, generally silent except when regaling us with stories of his childhood in the South, became my teacher, instructing me to seek solace, ironically, in the spoken word.

I didn't know it and perhaps he didn't either, but he was an orator in the style, and appearance, of Martin Luther King, Jr. He mastered intonation and dramatic pauses. A self-taught man who left school to work, Daddy began devouring the Bible and other religious texts. As every orator requires an audience, his stage became the church, his podium the pulpit. And in that scenario, he groomed me to follow his lead—to stand and speak, to lift myself and others with the power of the word.

In my home church and in neighboring churches, I spoke, my head inches above the podium. My speech written, I rarely needed its crutch. Words transcended mere sounds. They took cloth, shape, and form; and breathed life into my audiences, who were seated and applauding, nodding and smiling. That's when I first realized quite how powerful a solace public speaking could be.

Before my family and I moved to the South, when I visited my maternal grandparents' home as a girl, my siblings and cousins looked to me for not only consolation during times of sorrow in the family but also support and cheer on any given occasion. For us children, there were many hours to fill after a feast of an evening meal when the adults retired to the front porch to talk and laugh in the warm, mosquito-strummed air.

"Tootsie," my cousin Catty would say, excitement shining in her eyes, her hands tugging on my arm. "Tell us a story. Please, please!"

"Okay," I'd say, without too much pleading on my cousin's part, "but only if everyone will sit down and be quiet."

My directive was ever superfluous.

Once the other children understood that I was going to hold court with stories, they knew what to do. Orderly and quiet, my siblings (Big Sis, Bubba, Chicken, Glen, and the Baby Girl) formed a semi-circle around me, joined by my cousins, Catty, Bim, and Muff. No one whispered, breath suspended, the moment I began my spontaneous, original narrations. I knew the potency of the spoken word in their unblinking gaze, in their slightly parted lips, in their unmoving limbs. Even today, my cousin fondly remembers those long ago, storytelling visits.

My freshman year at Tuskegee Institute, I entered the "A Mind is a Terrible Thing to Waste" speech competition. I figured if my speaking prowess inspired and comforted my peers in my public-speaking class, surely it would serve me to enter the college's esteemed oratorical competition. And as with all of my speeches, my father supported me.

We discussed the topic, my intended sources, and the feelings I aimed to convey in the presentation. Once I outlined, drafted and revised the speech, I began practicing before Daddy after supper on the days I visited the homestead, when I wasn't ensconced in my campus dormitory, addressing mirrors aloud.

Excitement swirled the evening of the competition. Other competitors and I held tremulous hands in our laps, nervous at the pecking order for the night's flow. Around us, the campus chapel filled with distinguished faculty, community leaders, buzzing students, and participants' family members, who guided little ones to front pews. The building, a regal structure world famous, buzzed. Lights blazed. Organ music fired my feet, and when my name was called, I flew up the polished, winding wooden staircase to the podium, distended over the stage. I inhaled. Looked out on the audience and knew. And just like that, I became the words. The sentiments. The messages of Booker T. Washington, Frederick Douglass, and Ralph Ellison.

Although the first-place prize went to Pierre, a student with a French accent whose last name now evades me, I was a champion. I walked away having accomplished a close second place. Words had not failed me. Daddy, as most fathers probably might have argued in his shoes, deemed me the winner, saying all that my classmate had in his favor was his accent. But be that as it may, I knew solace in an extraordinary presence coursing through me from the moment I opened my mouth to the second I spoke my final word.

As an adult in the working world, words did my bidding.

An English teacher, I reveled in the beauty of words to charm my students and deepen their academic experiences throughout the year. In the solace of words, the students and I connected with contemporary and time-honored works. I taught them the intoxication of words by having them learn to appreciate the power of words to move, inflame, quell, provoke, romance, and persevere. We wrote original plays that we performed before the student body. We vied for and won speech competitions at local colleges, with me blazing the way by capturing first place and other honors in poetry, fiction and nonfiction in the community category. Many sat in Clark Atlanta's ceremonies as I read to high-school students, their teachers, college students, faculty, and community members.

Not surprisingly, I found solace in words outside of the classroom, as well.

As the English Department Head and coordinator of countless organizations from the Beta Club to the Senior Class, I addressed Black History at all-school assemblies. I spoke to audiences of English teachers at language and literature conferences on Jekyll Island and other places. I addressed English teachers in countywide meetings and at local schools. Later, after leaving the teaching profession, I worked for a while as a College Board consultant, who led SAT, PSAT, AP English and Fall Counselor workshops throughout the Southern region, and sometimes in other regions when there was a shortage of consultants. Joyously, through it all, words never failed me.

While in intimate relationships, I valued the necessity of de-plugging from a significant other to embrace myself. *I must go away to come again better than I was before*, a thought I once posted on my Facebook wall. The words resonated with so many others, who sent me private mesages to thank me for posting it. In my self-imposed solitude, my elixirs of choice were autobiographies, biographies, nonfiction, poetry books, and romance.

Sometimes my solace included others while I was in a relationship or while I was involved with someone I was dating. There is nothing more precious than being with someone special in a place ripe with words. When distance separated me from that person, I loved midnight conversations in which I read my poetry or prose to her. The music of the words and the ripeness of the mental space we shared were climactic. Attraction deepened. Though physical attraction has its place, the mental attraction sweetened with a sensual intoxication of the voice and words, I believe, strengthens human bonds. Likewise, to hear one's lover lost in the beauty of written or spoken words is an aphrodisiac. Not only is reading to one another an electric charge, but also just to read a book with a lover, to discuss it later, is paradise.

As a lesbian, I have sought solace in words when I didn't have a lover.

Lesbian autobiographical stories or their fictional romances were and are lifeboats that cruise me to other vistas, other emotional planes. There is something sacred in the stories of women daring to love one another in a world that hopes we do not exist, that flinches at the image of us being affectionate, that yet begrudges our couplings in a time of our legal marriages. We defy the odds when we love openly. It is necessary for us to be visible. We are here. We are meant to survive, we will survive, and we are surviving.

Long before I came out as a lesbian to myself, I was devouring lesbian words. In the solace of fictional worlds, I drew closer and closer to the proverbial closet door. Rosa Guy's *Ruby*, Nancy Garden's *Annie on My Mind*, Julie Ann Peters' *Keeping You a Secret*, Rita Mae Brown's *Ruby Fruit Jungle*, and Radclyffe Hall's *The Well of Loneliness* provided glimpses into the enchanting window of women loving women, a beautiful phenomenon I had, to that point, only witnessed on paper. In my mind, though, I transcended time and space to love women in consciousness, knowing its power to create the experiences for which I envisioned.

Later, I found my way to more reads that sustained my Sapphic desires in ways I'd never imagined possible. Suddenly, here were characters who reflected back to me glimpses of myself. I devoured Nikki Baker's *In the Game,* Cherry Muhanji's *Her: A Novel,* April Sinclair's *Coffee Will Make You Black*, Alice Walker's *The Color Purple*, Jewelle Gomez's *The Gilda Stories*, and Audre Lorde's *Sister Outsider: Essays and Speeches* and *Zami: A New Spelling of My Name*, amongst a plethora of other books.

I binged on young adult and children's classics by acclaimed lesbian writer Jacqueline Woodson, whose earlier work, the Maizon trilogy, as well as *The Dear One, From the Notebooks of Melanin Sun, Miracle's Boys,* and *If You Come Softly* enthralled me. Her stark prose and poetic narratives captured my attention for hours on end, and I introduced her to my charges. On countless afternoons, I read her work to the students, who never wanted me to pause in my reading. Moreover, Woodson's life seemed the enchantment of fairy tales. A Black lesbian living and loving her truth, while penning award-winning novels, she was a wellspring of inspiration, and when I learned that she was a friend of Linda Villarosa, who came out in the pages of *Essence*, I wrote Villarosa and Woodson to share my enthusiasm for their work and presence in the world.

My life-long love of words segued into a love for writing. After writing my first story in a spiral-bound notebook as an adolescent and sharing it with my first fan, my mother, I discovered a new solace in my own words. I began to fill more notebooks with stories and poetry. I drafted long, winding letters to friends I'd left behind in Waterbury. I penned detailed letters of the minutia of my days in epistles to family members. School essays were a delight. Much later, I wrote letters to the editors of local papers, an essay on natural beauty shining brightest in reference to the splendor of me loving my natural hair captured a spot in the *Atlanta Journal and Constitution*. In finding avenues to write for a larger audience while teaching, I wrote for the National Beta Club journals, and I covered feature stories for the local paper in Lithonia, GA.

When the Sterling McFadden Publishing Company was alive and well, I wrote countless un-bylined, first-person narratives to fill the pages of its cadre of magazines from *Black Romance*, *Jive* and *Black Secrets*. Fast forward the years, and I began publishing short stories in an assortment of magazines. *Players Magazine* accepted one. The magazine's accepting editor knew Ray Locke, an acquisitions editor at Holloway House. Locke read my story and called me, inquiring if I could make my story's main character, Dolly, live in 250 pages, and if I could, he'd send me a publishing contract. I agreed.

The rest is history. *Dolly: The Memoirs of a High School Graduate* was published in 1986. In the years that followed, I published stories and poems online and in several anthologies. Twelve years later, I self-published a romance novel, *If You Love Me, Come*. I followed that with a poetry collection, *Soft Tsunami*. Recently, my work has been anthologized in *Lez Talk: A Collection of Black Lesbian Fiction*. I am under contract with the BLF Press to write a short-story collection featuring Wanda B. Wonders, the contemporary counterpart, I like to think, to Langston Hughes' Jess B. Simple. Like Simple, Wanda ponders life in two colors: black and white.

In short, I yet seek solace in words, written and spoken, and I do not ever want to fathom a time when I am not using words to comfort myself and others in times of distress or sadness and using words to cheer and support others, as we make our way on our extraordinary journeys.

What does it take to build an empire

Imani Sims

rainbow wasp nest
resilient cluster sting
low hum steady
fluttered wing yellow
lit. emblazoned belly
over twisted waist
steady march forward.

we know
librecht baker

in thirst, we tug ropes attached to buckets at well's
bottom, holding liters of our oratory we orate
spitting reed and brass blown improv kicking
language like dixieland music

we kick belief as if it were dissipating dust,
forgetting we is real

within us is medicine needing tutelage so fear,
fight, and flight aren't first responses

within we is lineage, an internal elder currenting
tapestry in our speak

we speak these blueprints as reverence for now as
though it was before, before

supplying our matter with matter like we matter as
those before

our body is first land is matter is making memory
is tomorrow's recollections

we recall self-permission and bless it so we birth
again and again

permitting passage to our rites of passage to
become dreams' passage

rite the storm, spread its waters upon which ever
fields holler for growth, we run deep

institutions don't cultivate what we sow, we
channel worlds

we cultivate when and wherever we enter and
burn what needs not be intact

making impact with language seen as mumbo
jumbo, but its mumbo is coded

bursts of essence falling prostrate before our rise,
blessed be our openings

now is the time to converge upon our advantage
of being here

without a dirge for tomorrow, now is our foundation

for tomorrow is too far away, let's make moves with the gleam of what we know

we know self-doubt so let it pass as clouds, it shall pass, it shall pass, it shall pass

allow this strange season to pass in deep breaths with intention and action

the effect of self-will is season of fruits so reference feelings as wisdom

wisdom is our being, our technology, our academy, our alphabet, and beyond here

since we must commune in alphabets, let us intend to libate ourselves in reverie

and continuously dream our flight until we see multiple landings and glide life

there are light years within us, we are affluent resources

beyond bank notes, we need courage to liberate ourselves

although we appear to birth and die alone, we testify to our comings and goings

taking notes, making books of our notes, libraries of our books, institutes of our libraries

never is a time to wait and what we know is the first bar of gold.

"we know self-doubt so let it pass as clouds,
it shall pass, it shall pass, it shall pass"

Works Cited

Anzaldúa, Gloria. *Borderlands/ La Frontera*. San Francisco: Aunt Lute, 1999. Print.

Maso, Carole. *Break Every Rule: Essays on Language, Longing, & Moments of Desire* Counterpoint, 2000.

Miłosz, Czesław. *Szukanie ojczyzny* (*In Search of a Homeland*); Kraków: Społeczn Instytut Wydawniczy Znak (1992).

Shadowlands. Directed by Richard Attenborough, performances by Anthony Hopkins, Debra Winger. Price Entertainment, 1994.

Contributors

S. Andrea Allen

S. (Stephanie) Andrea Allen, Ph.D., is a native southerner and out Black lesbian writer, scholar, and educator. Her works in progress include *A Failure to Communicate*, a collection of short fiction and essays. Her other writing credits include scholarly articles on the topics of race and sexuality, and work as a reviewer for *Feral Feminisms* and The Lesbrary.

In 2014, Stephanie founded BLF Press, and her first edited collection, *Lez Talk: A Collection of Black Lesbian Short Fiction,* was released in the spring of 2016. She co-founded the bi-weekly radio show, Lez Talk Books Radio, which aims to amplify the writing of Black lesbians; and the Black Lesbian Literary Collective, a non-profit "collaborative effort among women with shared cultural experiences who desire a nurturing and productive writing setting." Stephanie is also a founding board member of the Bay Area Lesbian Archives.

Hala Aurangzeb

Anti-racist activist, writer, and youth advocate in Vancouver, BC.

librecht baker

librecht baker. Dembrebrah West African Drum & Dance Ensemble member. Adjunct Instructor at Los Angeles Southwest College. VONA/Voices & Lambda Literary Fellow. Sundress Publications' Assistant Editor. MFA in Interdisciplinary Arts from Goddard College. Poetry in *Writing the Walls Down: A Convergence of LGBTQ Voices*, *CHORUS: A Literary Mixtape*, and *Emgere*: 2015 Lambda Literary Fellows Anthology. Currently, birthing and manifesting.

Kendra N. Bryant

Kendra N. Bryant is an assistant professor of English at the University of North Georgia-Oconee. She has been teaching writing for 16 years and engages in her own writing practice via her blogging space at: drknbryant.com.

Eliana Buenrostro

Eliana Buenrostro is a writer, Chicana and spiritual activist. She was born and raised in Southern California and is currently based in Chicago.

Lauren Cherelle

Lauren Cherelle uses her time and talents to traverse imaginary and professional worlds. She manages and writes for Resolute Publishing, an indie publisher that helps transform dreams into realities for female writers. Her second novel, *The Dawn of Nia*—a story about the sting of abandonment, the difficulty of forgiveness, and the grace of transformative love—was released in April 2016. She has published stories in *G.R.I.T.S: Girls Raised in the South: An Anthology of Queer Womyn's Voices & Their Allies* (2013) and *Lez Talk: A Collection of Black Lesbian Short Fiction* (2016). Find her online at www.lcherelle.com.

M. Shelly Conner

M. Shelly Conner is Chicago-based writer, humorist, and scholar. Her writing has appeared in *The Feminist Wire*, *xoJane*, *Black Girl Dangerous*, *Skin to Skin Magazine*, and *The Frisky*. Shelly's comedy webseries, *Quare Life*, is in development with OpenTV. She is currently exploring publishing options for her debut novel everyman (forthcoming excerpt in *Obsidian Journal of Literature of the African Diaspora*). She is Executive Director of Quare Square Collective, Inc.— a 501(c)(3) non-profit for queer artists of color. Follow her blog about travel, culture and food through queer womanist of color lens at dappervista.tumblr.com.

Eunice Gonzalez-Sierra

Eunice Gonzalez-Sierra is a Mexican-American who first arrived to the United States in the belly of her immigrant mother. She was raised in Santa Maria, CA where her parents immigrated to and dedicated their lives to picking one of the sweetest fruits in the world, strawberries. She is passionate about social justice, writing, and exuding lots of self-love. While an undergraduate at UCLA, Eunice was a part of UCLA's Spoken Word Space, "The Word on Wednesday's," where she performed many of her writing pieces and found the power in her voice (even when it shook). With a Bachelor's degree in Chicana/o Studies, she hopes to continue spreading consciousness and kindness through her words and the love for her people, remembering that "your silence will not protect you."

Claudia Moss

Claudia Moss is a novelist, poet, speaker, blogger, vlogger and content creator. She is the author of two novels, *Dolly: The Memoirs of a High School Graduate* and *If You Love Me, Come*. Claudia is the creator of *The Wanda B. Wonders* series, which features the feisty Ms. Wanda B. Wonders, who renders her life in two colors, black and white. Claudia is also the author of *Soft Tsunami*, a poetry collection.

Her stories appear in the new anthology, *Lez Talk: A Collection of Black Lesbian Short Fiction*.

Nik Nicholson

Nik Nicholson is an author, poet, content editor, book formatter, writing coach, painter and education performer. Her short stories and poems are featured in several anthologies. Her first novel, *Descendants of Hagar*, won the 2013 Lambda Literary LGBT Debut Fiction Award. It's the first of a two-part series, which also includes *Daughter of Zion*, about a woman coming to terms with her masculinity in the early 1900's.

In 2015, Nicholson was awarded the Regional Artist Support Grant for 2015, which funded research in Harlem for her second novel, *Daughter of Zion*. *Daughter of Zion* is scheduled to be released in the summer of 2017.

Web home: http://www.niknicholson.com
Facebook: http://www.facebook.com/ArtistNik
Twitter: http://www.twitter.com/artistnikn
Blog: https://niknicholson.wordpress.com

Almah LaVon Rice

Almah LaVon Rice has been published in various anthologies, including *The Ringing Ear: Black Poets Lean South*, *Black Quantum Futurism: The-*

ory & Practice (Volume 1), and the revised edition of *does your mama know?: Black Lesbian Coming Out Stories.* Her journalism has garnered a National Ethnic Media Award from New America Media and recognition on Utne Reader's "Great Writing" blog. She served as the programming co-chair for Fire & Ink IV: Witness, a writers' conference for LGBTQ and SGL writers of African descent.

In addition to being an Artist-in-Residence at Howard University Hospital through the Smith Farm for the Healing Arts, Almah's other residencies include the School for Designing A Society, Blue Mountain Center, and Wells College. She has presented workshops at Organizing Neighborhood Equity (Washington, DC) and the African American Women's Resource Center (Washington, DC); Free University (Gainesville, FL); Indigo Days (Durham, NC); and Poetry Jam at the College of Santa Fe (Santa Fe, NM); and the Black Lesbian Conference (Los Angeles, CA), among others.

Almah's installation work has been featured at the Transmodern Festival in Baltimore, and she is currently exploring expressive abstract painting. Residing in Westsylvania, she is also at work on a spellbook of black folk magic and fictions.

Imani Sims

Imani Sims is a spicy Chai tea loving Seattle native who spun her first performance poem at the age of fourteen. Since then, she has developed an infinitely rippling love for poetry in all of its forms. She believes in the healing power of words and the transformational nuance of the human story. Imani works to empower youth and adults through various writing courses and interdisciplinary shows all over Washington. She is a 2016 CityArtist Grant recipient, Central District Forum for Arts and Ideas curator, and Gay City Arts Fellow where she brought Afrofuturism and Performance Art together for eight shows. Her book, *(A)live Heart*, is forthcoming on Sibling Rivalry Press this fall.

Mica Standing Soldier

Mica Standing Soldier is an Oglala Lakota woman majoring in English and Creative Writing at the University of Minnesota - Twin Cities.

She's currently the chair of the Minnesota Public Interest Research Group, community outreach coordinator for Take Back the Night Twin Cities, and founder of the Coalition Against Mass Incarceration. She works to eradicate violence against LGBTQ-POC and promote social justice and equity for marginalized peoples.

Dr. Nubian Sun

Dr. Nubian Sun, LCSW, Social Work Teacher-Scholar, Activist, and Spirit-Filled Practitioner, is a native of Memphis, TN. She is currently an Assistant Professor of Social Work at WKU. She earned her Bachelor's in Social Work from the University of Tennessee-Chattanooga and received her Master's degree in Social Work-Community Welfare Management from the University of Tennessee-Knoxville (Nashville Campus). She completed her Doctorate degree in Social Work Policy, Planning and Administration at the Whitney M. Young Jr., School of Social Work at Clark Atlanta University in March 2015. Her practice, pedagogy and scholarship interests include: the Afrocentric perspective, reentry, self-efficacy, performance and social justice, and the intersections of reproductive justice. As an Artivist and Spirit-Filled Practitioner, she travels between the worlds of theater, culinary arts, African Diasporic dance and drumming, visual/ abstract art, healing arts, and music.

Sheila Tartaglia

Sheila Tartaglia is an African American writer, poet, lifelong feminist, lifelong learner, and business owner. Frequently traversing "roads less traveled," she honors her life's powerful and unique journey through her poetry and prose, which has appeared in numerous publications. An avid gardener, Sheila loves to plant trees and perennials each year that she knows will continue to grow and blossom long after she is gone. Her deep belief in the adage "Sisterhood is Powerful" continues to inform her life and bring joy to her heart. Sheila has been married for 27 years and counting.

Photo Credits

CPSIA information can be obtained
at www.ICGtesting.com
Printed in the USA
FSOW04n0509070117
29212FS